D1328797

I AM THE
MINOTAUR

ANTHONY
McGOWAN

OXFORD
UNIVERSITY PRESS

Barrington Stoke

Great Clarendon Street, Oxford, OX2 6DP, United Kingdom

Oxford University Press is a department of the University of Oxford.

It furthers the University's objective of excellence in research, scholarship, and education by publishing worldwide. Oxford is a registered trade mark of Oxford University Press in the UK and in certain other countries

British Library Cataloguing in Publication Data

Data available

ISBN 978-0-19-8494874

1 3 5 7 9 10 8 6 4 2

Paper used in the production of this book is a natural, recyclable product made from wood grown in sustainable forests.

The manufacturing process conforms to the environmental regulations of the country of origin.

Printed in China by Golden Cup

Acknowledgements

Cover: Oxford University Press / Shutterstock

The publisher would like to thank Jane Branson for writing the additional resources.

To all the young carers

Chapter 1

Who Is Stinky Mog?

Stinky Mog was a kid at my school. There's a Stinky Mog at your school, too, I bet. You probably don't call him Stinky Mog, but he's there, on the edge of things, in the shadows.

At my school, just like yours, there were groups and gangs and cliques. Kids who were in, and kids who were out.

You could see the school as a circle, with some kids at the centre, like the sun, and some at the outer rim, like Pluto, going around alone in the cold and the dark. Or you could see it as layers. Like a cake, maybe. No, not a cake. More like a pond, with the fast and beautiful fish swimming around at the top, near the light, and then the duller and weaker fish further down. Finally there was the slime and the filth at the bottom, where the dead things were, and the things that might as well be dead.

That was Stinky Mog. He was puny planet Pluto, freezing his nuts off in the outer dark. He was the slime-dweller, slithering in the filth at the bottom of the pond. He didn't have any friends. Because to be friends with Stinky Mog would make you stinky, too. And who wants that? It's a stink you can't wash off.

How did Stinky Mog become Stinky Mog? Or was he always Stinky Mog, born into the slime?

No, there was a time when things were OK for Stinky Mog. Before his mum lost it. Before his mum lost herself. Stinky Mog remembered birthday parties with other kids and cake and presents, and his mum laughing, her hair golden in the sunlight. But gradually he drifted into the darkness.

What happened?

Stinky Mog didn't know. He was only a kid. Grown-ups are complicated. But first his mum stopped picking him up from school and he had to walk back alone. The other mums and dads at the school gates would look at Stinky Mog and then at each other as he began the walk back in the rain. But they never said anything.

Stinky Mog's mum couldn't walk very well any more. For a while she had a stick. And then she got a mobility scooter that lived in the downstairs hall of their block of flats. Stinky Mog hated that scooter and was terrified the other kids at junior school would see his mum on it. He knew what they'd say. He knew they'd laugh at her and him.

Stinky Mog's mum went out less and less, and then she stopped going out at all. She just sat on the settee all day, watching the telly. Soon she stopped changing out of her night clothes. Or rather her day clothes and her night clothes became the same thing. Stinky Mog was only a kid, still just seven or eight years old, but he had to go to the shop on the corner to buy food with the money his mum put into his small hand.

The man in the shop always looked at the money, shook his head and put some things in a bag: bread and milk and tea and margarine and sometimes ham and cheese. And one special time the man put in a bunch of grapes that were going bad – a kind, not cruel, act. He patted Stinky Mog's greasy head and said, "Get some vitamins in you so you can do some growing." Stinky Mog's mum was never unkind, and she let him eat all the grapes.

3

They went off like hand grenades of happiness in his mouth, the nicest thing he'd ever tasted.

And when Stinky Mog grew, his clothes stayed the same size, as they weren't magical clothes like in a fairy tale. The clothes were not clean. That was when the other kids at his junior school started to call him Stinky Mog. And by naming him this, they made it real. There was no Stinky Mog before the name. But after the name, there was only Stinky Mog. The kids even made up a song:

Stinky Mog
Stinky Mog
He looks like a tramp
And he smells like a bog.

Stinky Mog
Stinky Mog
I'd rather snog a skunk
Or a smelly dog.

The song, and the laughter, followed Stinky Mog around for a few days until the teachers stopped it. And then it lived on as a whisper, a memory, a threat.

The teachers at the school were nice. One of them brought Stinky Mog some old clothes to wear. And the dinner lady gave him second helpings, as she saw how he gazed at the food with such longing, even when it was only dry fish fingers or grey cottage pie or rubbery pizza.

So in term-time at least, Stinky Mog didn't starve.

But he did stink.

There was a washing machine in their flat, but it didn't work. Stinky Mog had a memory of his mother putting clothes in the round glass door, like a window on a ship, and pressing buttons. Once he tried to do the same, but nothing happened. No lights came on, and the drum inside did not turn. He took the clothes out again and wore them the next day.

People came to see Stinky Mog and his mum. Men in suits. Ladies in suits. When they came, his mum changed, snapped out of it. She became more like the mum he remembered. Before they arrived she would comb his hair and wipe his face and say, "Right, let's make you smart for the council."

But after they had gone, his mum would lie down again on the settee.

"Make us a cup of tea, love," she'd say, and he would, because there was always tea and often milk, even when there was nothing else.

The less that Mum did, the more Stinky Mog had to do. As well as the shopping, he was soon doing the cooking. Not that he was any good at it. His cooking was mainly toast. And he did the cleaning. Well, he tried to make the place look tidy at least. After a time, the hoover broke, so the carpet was basically just dust held together with fluff.

There were still some days when Stinky Mog's mum was nice. They'd sit together and watch the old telly, and she'd put her arm around him and stroke his greasy hair.

And once his mum said, "Poo, you need a bath," and she took him to the bathroom and ran the water, but the water was cold. So then she boiled kettle after kettle until the water was warm, and she put some washing-up liquid in the water because there wasn't any soap or shampoo. Stinky Mog got in and washed away the dirt and the smell, and it felt really nice.

As he grew older, Stinky Mog learned how to get by. The water was nearly always cold, but he would wash his hands and face in the sink. And sometimes he would put his dirty clothes in the cold bath, squirt washing-up liquid in the water and stamp about on them until the water turned grey.

But still, it was hard for Stinky Mog not to be dirty and not to be stinky. And still, when the teacher left the room, the other kids would sing the Stinky Mog song, especially if he had done something stupid, like getting noticed. The pain of it and the shame of it burned him, and shrivelled him, and made it so that the only thing he wanted in the world was to be invisible.

And then Stinky Mog came to the end of junior school, and he was scared and hopeful at the same time. His mum came out of her secret world, briefly, to somehow buy him the basics of the secondary school uniform: a sweatshirt and a pair of black trousers. She bought them, sensibly, in sizes far too big. (Though in time Stinky Mog outgrew them. Then he would tug at his sleeves so that his grey-white wrists might not be exposed, and pull at his trousers to encourage them over his ankles.)

Stinky Mog's first two days at secondary school were fine. The great thing was that none of the kids from his year at junior school had gone on to this school. It was a miracle, almost. It meant he could start again. Stinky Mog knew that all he had to do was stay below the radar, not get noticed.

At lunch he sat at a big table, close enough to some other kids in his class so he didn't seem completely on his own. Stinky Mog was too shy to talk to anyone, but that didn't matter. He didn't look too different to the others. He was just one kid in a mass of kids. They were all shy and a bit scared.

On the second day a boy asked him to pass the salt and said, "Thanks." It was a small thing, but Stinky Mog let himself hope. Maybe he would have a friend here.

And then, on the third day, he heard it. Stinky Mog was in the schoolyard, sitting on one of the concrete benches. He was reading a book he'd got from the school library. It was about rabbits. Sounds stupid, but it was a good book. The rabbits lived in a warren that was going to be destroyed, and so some of them escaped and tried to find a new safe place to live. It was exciting. And there was a kind, clever, brave rabbit who looked after the others – the crap rabbits. Stinky Mog was thinking it would be OK to be a rabbit, even if you had to watch out for foxes and weasels and men with guns.

It was then that he heard it, when he was still inside his own head, thinking about the rabbits and their adventures. It was quiet to begin with – just one voice, hardly more than a whisper. But then it grew louder, first that one voice, but then others joining in, until the sound of it in his head was like a football crowd.

Stinky Mog
Stinky Mog
He looks like a tramp
And he smells like a bog.

Stinky Mog
Stinky Mog
I'd rather snog a skunk
Or a smelly dog.

So, it had happened. The song had come with Stinky Mog to secondary school, clinging to him like the old stink.

He looked up from his book. There was a kid there, a small one – more weasel than fox. The kid had a joyous light of evil shining in his eyes. Stinky Mog recognised him. This kid had been in the year ahead of him at junior school.

It wasn't fair.

It wasn't fair.

It wasn't fair.

Chapter 2

I Am Stinky Mog

Who am I kidding?

You've guessed it already.

You know.

Everyone knows.

Stinky Mog wasn't a kid at my school. *I* was Stinky Mog. Stinky Mog was me. There are some things you just can't hide.

It wasn't fair that the song followed me. Nothing is fair. I learned to live with it. Learned to live with being Stinky Mog. Some time went by. I coped. The song followed me for the first year. It followed and I ran. And I hid. The song stopped any chance of friendship. But that was fine. What's bad is hope. Hope is what kills you. So if you can kill hope, then you're OK.

I got good at being invisible. It's a skill – like juggling or shoplifting. You've got to practise.

Let me tell you some more about my school. Everyone said it was a good school. And they were right. Kids wanted to come here. Or, rather, parents wanted their kids to go there. Kids here got good results. They didn't leave school and then go straight onto benefits. They went to good universities. They ended up with the good jobs, the ones everyone wanted. Same as their mums and dads.

So this wasn't one of those schools where the thick kids and the hard kids preyed on the rest, the way lions and wolves prey on smaller creatures. In this school you didn't get some big lump the size of a fridge come up to you and punch you down and then steal your phone and stamp on your face while his mates laughed like hyenas. You got the odd fight, but it was just what they call "handbags" – two kids flapping at each other without doing any damage.

But there are other ways of getting hurt, other ways of bleeding.

Like I said, this school had various gangs and in-groups, and sometimes it seemed that every kid was in one of them but me.

There were the sporty kids, who all walked with a bounce, as if gravity didn't apply to them in the same way it did to the rest of us. It was like they were made of different stuff, some shiny new metal as light as it was strong. Not just aircraft aluminium, like iPhones, but space aluminium, designed for starships.

Then there were the brainiacs. In some schools they'd be the geeks and goofs with thick glasses and buck teeth, always looking behind them for the next attack. But here nobody minded them. The teachers loved the brainiacs, of course, because they'd get the good grades, reflecting glory on the school and on them. But even the other kids accepted them, which was weird. In fact, they "got" the brainiacs. Wanted to be them.

Then there were the artsy kids, the drama-club gang, who sang in the choir and played the violin and starred in the summer play and the winter musical. They always looked happy, draping themselves over each other, boys and girls all jumbled up so you couldn't tell which was which.

I watched them sometimes and wished that I could be there, in the middle of that laughing mass of arms and legs.

And at this school even the outsiders were insiders. There were goth kids, mixing into emo, with black nails and white faces. These kids should've got regular spankings from the thugs, except we didn't have thugs, and no one else could be bothered to bother them. Maybe sometimes a random kid would shout out "EMO!", but the goths would stare them out or just shrug and get back to the job of being them.

I wished I was one of them, too. Part of that solid wall of white and black facing the world, keeping out the wind and the rain.

So you had all these groups, these gangs – but don't think gangs like the gangs on our estate, because none of these kids carried a knife in their inside pocket. I just mean gangs like a group.

But there was one last group. They didn't have a name. They had a colour – gold – and a smell, which was like flowers and grass. And probably even a taste, which would be sweet and … rich. Their parents worked in the media – TV, or music, or online. These kids didn't go on about it much – they didn't have to.

At the core of this group were Si, Moll, Ari and Ez. There were others, others just as golden, or almost as golden. But these four kids were the ones that counted. And they were OK. They didn't pick on Stinky Mog, didn't sing the song. They were above that. They didn't even "see" him. He just didn't exist for them. I mean me – sorry. It was me that they didn't notice.

But I noticed them. In particular, Ari ...

Chapter 3

Ariadne

Three, four years of secondary school went by. Stinky Mog was Stinky Mog again. He ... no, I – I sat on my own at lunch. Every day. Every lunch. I took my tray and found a table by the wall with no one there. I sat on my own at break. I sat wherever no one else was. I was the shadow by the wall. I was the shape that left the room just when other people came in. An absence, not a presence.

I tried to keep myself clean. I tried not to look terrible. And often I failed. My uniform grew more ragged with the years, and there were holes in the sleeves of my jumper, so I rolled them up.

How often did I get called Stinky Mog? Not often. The teachers called me Matthew. Nobody else called me anything much. But sometimes it would come. I'd be sitting on my own at break and a football would roll my way, and someone would shout, "Oi, Stinky Mog, pass us the ball back!" Sometimes the other kids would laugh, and sometimes not. I don't think they even knew why they called me Stinky Mog.

Was it hell? No. You get used to stuff. Home. School. You get used to them.

I saw a documentary once about these pools fed by water that comes bubbling up from deep in the earth. It's nearly boiling, yet it's got life in it: shrimps and little fishes. The water should cook them, but they've got used to the heat.

And sometimes Mum would wake up. I don't mean wake up from sleep, but I do, sort of. I mean she'd suddenly be herself again, and she'd notice me and see that I was a mess. Then we'd go to the charity shop, her riding that terrible mobility scooter with me cringing by the side of her, and she'd find me a new pair of trousers or a shirt or whatever.

So that was me, and the school, and the everything of my life. It was bad. But like the shrimps in the boiling water, I'd got used to it.

Then something happened.

Ari.

Short for Ariadne, who was a Greek goddess. No, a princess. A teacher at junior school had read us stories from the Greek myths, and I remembered them all. Ariadne was a princess from Crete. Her dad was King Minos. A Greek hero called Theseus went to Crete and had to kill a monster. This half man, half bull was called the Minotaur, and he lived in a maze called the Labyrinth. Ariadne helped Theseus, giving him a sword so he could kill the Minotaur, and some thread so he could find his way out of the Labyrinth. Theseus sailed away from Crete with Ariadne, but then he dumped her on some other island because he didn't love her. Nutter.

I always felt sorry for the Minotaur. He was trapped in the Labyrinth. He didn't choose to be a monster. Who does?

I had a few classes with Ari – English and History and Physics. She sat in the middle, one row back, with Si, Moll and Ez. And the gold of these kids made a kind of haze. The golden gang didn't notice me, but I noticed them. Well, in particular, Ari. I sat at the back and watched Ari move her hair behind her ear, or scratch the tip of her nose, or bounce her pencil off her bottom lip. When the teacher asked a question, Ari would wait a moment to give someone else a chance to answer. But when no one moved she would put that long arm in the air, with her wrist bent back a bit. The teacher would say, "Tell us, Ari," and Ari would. And her voice was so beautiful I could never hear the words but just the music of it.

I was OK at English. I like reading. I like trying to turn the ideas in my head into words on the paper. But I never said anything in English class. Even when I knew the answer I always kept my hand down. The last thing I needed was every face turning towards me while I stammered out some words. Eyes staring, seeing, judging. It was safer to stay silent.

English lessons were the best time to look at Ari. It was only then that I could properly – what's the word? – *gaze* at her. Other times, I couldn't risk it – in the yard, the corridors, the canteen. Couldn't take the chance. What if someone saw me staring at her? The truth was only safe when it was closed up in the lead box that was my heart. My true feelings were like radiation. If they got out, if they leaked, I would die.

So I longed and I yearned for Ari, and there was a kind of happiness in this, weirdly. These feelings were so much better than everything else in my life. Everything else was cold and dark, but they were warm and golden. It was all I needed.

And then it changed.

Chapter 4

Birthday

It was after an English lesson. The golden gang were leaving the classroom, chatting away. I normally waited till everyone had gone so I could slip out quietly. But they were talking so much, loitering, laughing.

"You've got to do *something*!"

That was Si. Si was what every boy wanted to be. Tall, handsome, chilled. Nothing was difficult for him. He got on with everyone – had the right smile, the right word for each person he spoke to.

I hated him.

"Yeah, how can you do nothing?" This was Moll speaking. "I mean, you can do nothing any time you want. Doing nothing is easy."

Moll was neat and dark, and her expression was always turned up to the max – happy or sad or excited or bored. It was as if she were demonstrating these things to an alien who knew nothing about human feelings.

Ari tossed her head back and laughed. It looked to me like her laugh wasn't completely natural. It was one of those laughs with effort in it.

"Look," Ari said, "I just want tomorrow to be a normal day. I hate fuss. Hate being the centre of things. I don't want any presents. There's nothing I need. There's enough ... stuff in my life. I know – Si, you write me one of your poems. Moll, do me a drawing. Ez, make me laugh."

"Girl, you are too good to be true," said Ez, putting on an American accent.

Ez was always doing voices – Scottish or Irish or American or Russian. In fact I wasn't sure what his own true voice was like. Ez was the joker, but the laughs he got were for the accents, for how he said things, not for *what* he said.

"At least you've got to have a party," said Moll. She pulled an astonished face – as if anyone could see that this was the right thing to do. "Not tomorrow but at the weekend."

"Yeah, house party," said Ez. "House party! House party!"

Ari appeared suddenly unsure. She shook her head, and I thought she was going to say something, but she just looked down.

"Shut up, Ez," Si said with a smile, but a smile that had steel at the heart of it. "Thing about your birthday is that you can do what you want." Si touched Ari lightly on the arm. Just his fingers, not his whole hand. Somehow the fingers made it more intimate, closer. "It's cool, Ari."

Ari put her hand up to her arm and touched Si's fingers, which were still resting there.

Did I mention that I hated Si?

And then they spilled out of the room, and after a few seconds I followed.

*

So, it was Ari's birthday tomorrow. Something small and mean in me was glad that she wasn't going to have a party. Glad because I wouldn't be invited, obviously. Glad because I didn't want to think of it happening with me not there, and Si's fingers on her arm, and the laughter and the happiness.

I imagined the whole scene: me wandering around the streets, coming across the sound of a party, following it. I'd see the bright lights from her house – a big house, the kind that posh people live in – and go up to it and look in the window. And the light in there, the happiness, the colours, the warmth. I'd always been on the outside with rain falling on me.

But then I thought, *Stop feeling sorry for yourself. Stinky Mog has put up with worse than this.* And another thought grew in my mind. Ari didn't want a birthday party, didn't want a fuss. I liked her for that, which was weird, because I thought my, er, *liking* of her was already up to the limit, right at the top – no room for any more in the bottle. But it turns out that feelings aren't like that. They don't understand limits. They can go on, go up, forever.

And I thought about what Ari had wanted from her friends. Not the sort of things that needed money.

A song.

A joke.

A poem.

Maybe I could ...

No. Stupid. Who would want a poem from Stinky Mog? Who would want a joke from him?

He was the joke. And a song? There was only one song.

Stinky Mog
Stinky Mog
He looks like a ...

Chapter 5

The Minotaur Writes a Poem

My mum was bad that night. When I got in from school, she was lying on the settee. The flat was freezing. And there was an odd damp smell, like when you stroke a street dog and then sniff your hand. We couldn't put the heating on. There wasn't any money for it.

"Are you OK, Mum?" I said.

She turned her eyes towards me. She had cushions piled over her, for warmth I suppose. It looked almost funny, like she'd built a pillow fort for herself.

"Make us a cup of tea, love," Mum said, her voice flat.

There wasn't any milk, so I made the tea black. I put a splash of cold water in so it didn't scald her mouth when she drank it. I put the mug on the floor next to the settee. Then I went and got the duvet from her bed, moved the cushions out of the way and put it over her.

You probably want to know what was wrong with my mum, like, was it cancer or heart disease or whatever. People want there to be a thing. If there's a thing you can go, *Ah! That explains it, that's why she's like that.* But there isn't always a thing. Or, sometimes the thing is so complicated it isn't really a thing at all, but things. And sometimes it's everything.

So, my mum didn't have a physical thing wrong with her. Well, she had a dodgy hip, but that wasn't the real problem. The real problem was depression and anxiety and sadness. And poverty. Her life was rubbish, broken, and she didn't know how to make it better. Her life, our life. My life.

There was a packet of noodles in the cupboard. The kind that come with a small foil sachet of flavouring. I boiled the noodles and sprinkled the powder into the pan and then licked the foil to get an intense hit of savoury flavour. There were the crusts from a sliced white loaf. No butter or spread. I divided up the noodles and crusts and brought Mum's half to her on a tray. We watched the soaps together. After a while I saw her eyelids droop, and I went to do my homework in my room, getting under the covers to keep warm. Later on I went to check on her.

"Let's get you to bed, Mum," I said.

"Think I'll stay here tonight," she replied. "Sick of that room. Comfy here."

"OK."

I brought Mum's pillow and tucked her in on the settee. Before I left her she grabbed my hand and said, "You're a good boy, Matthew."

"I love you, Mum," I said.

I don't know where that came from. I hadn't said it for a long time. Sometimes I hated my mum and blamed her for everything. But that hate wasn't true. It was like when you bash your toe, and you hate your toe for hurting so much. But you don't really hate your toe. So the hate was a lie, but the love was true. It would probably have been easier if it were the other way round. Loving hurts much more than hating. And when you hate something you can walk away from it or shut it out of your mind. But you can't do that with love. Love is always there. Always there.

When I said the words, my mum's face changed as if she'd felt a stab of pain. I thought she was going to cry, and I had to get out of there because I couldn't stand that.

*

That night I tried to think up a poem – a poem for Ari. It took me hours. I did about ten versions. This was the best one:

> Ariadne, your hero will desert you
> On some far-distant shore.
> The one whose love was true
> Was not Theseus, but the Minotaur.

It was rubbish. There was something wrong with the rhythm, but I couldn't fix it. At least it rhymed.

My mum had a drawer with cards and stuff in – old Christmas and birthday cards that we hadn't sent, that sort of thing. They'd been there for years, going back to when Mum had a better grip on life. I got up. I could hear Mum breathing heavily on the settee. She mumbled a few words, but nothing I could understand.

I found a card with a pattern of stars and rainbows on the front. Inside it said, CONGRATULATIONS!!! I think it was a sort of all-purpose card, for when you have a baby or get married or divorced or whatever. But it was the best I could do.

I wrote my poem out on the card in my best writing and sealed it up, then wrote ARIADNE on the outside. I used capitals so Ari wouldn't recognise my handwriting. But that was stupid: as if she'd ever have noticed what my handwriting was like.

I didn't think I'd ever give the dumb poem to Ari, but it made me feel sort of happy that I'd written it. There was a compact neatness to the card sealed up in the envelope, and it felt good in my hand.

Chapter 6

The Locker of Doom

The next day was a weird one. I had one class with Ari – Physics. I thought the golden gang would be buzzing about her birthday, but nobody was talking about it. I thought maybe Ari looked a bit sad about that. You know how when you tell people not to make a fuss about something and then they don't? And that pisses you off? Well, I didn't know about that, because I had no one to tell, but you know what I mean.

I had the card with the poem in my bag. Of course I wasn't just going to give it to Ari. I was Stinky Mog not Mad Mog. But there was an easy way to get it to her. We all had lockers. The lockers had metal doors with enough of a gap at the bottom to slip a card in. I couldn't do it at break, as there were always kids hanging around the lockers. Even if Ari didn't catch me doing it, someone might see me and tell her, and then Stinky Mog would be exposed.

I saw a YouTube clip once of this sea turtle that had been caught by some fishermen. It was a giant, prehistoric-looking thing – the size of a bath, but helpless out of the water. You thought the fishermen were just going to kill it. But what they did was cut it out of its shell with these long knives like machetes and then they just left it there on the floor. The turtle had this look on its face – a sort of baffled hopelessness. Because a turtle just has this one thing to save it, the shell. Without the shell it's got nothing. Just the soft pink stuff where the shell used to be.

And if Ari found out I'd written the poem, that would be me.

So I hung around as the lessons changed over, waiting for the corridors to empty. Then I scurried down to the lockers, which were in a sort of basement area near the gym. There were a couple of scabby Year 7s there, looking shifty, like they were doing something sneaky, but they were probably just late for lessons.

There's a thing that people like me do sometimes, I mean people near the bottom of the pond. They try to find someone below even them and pass the grief on down. In school, the way this works is that even the lowest kid in a year beats the top kids in the year below. That's just the way it is. That's the truth of it. The science of it. So, anyway, I wasn't a slime-dweller as far as these midgets were concerned – no, sir, I was this dangerous, unpredictable Year 9 ogre.

But I didn't do that. Not normally. I mean, passing on grief, like it was a disease. I just ignored the small fry, like I wanted to be ignored in return.

But that day was different. I had a job to do. So I made a sort of growling noise and said, "Get lost" to these kids. They hadn't even seen me up until then, so I had surprise on my side. I thought the Year 7s might crap themselves, they looked so scared. They scuttled out of there like cockroaches.

Now you're probably wondering how I even knew which locker belonged to Ari, but if you are wondering that, then it means you've never been in ... it means you've never had *feelings*. Because when you have feelings, you know these things. You know when the person you've got feelings for has some new trainers. You know when they've changed their hair. You know when they've bought some new nail varnish, because it's a slightly different shade of red, paler and less intense …

And you damn well know what number their locker is. It's like a super-sense. If you don't, you aren't in … you don't have those feelings.

So I went to her locker, number 362. A magical number. A beautiful number. Every part of it was perfect. That 3, friendly and round and wanting to make you happy. The 6, like a guardian, looking after the others, kind of like a big brother. And best of all the 2, elegant 2, perfect 2.

I took the envelope out of my bag, hesitated for a moment, looked around, hesitated some more, then slipped it under the locker door. A corner of the envelope peeked out. That was no good. One of Ari's friends would see it and ask her what it was, then they'd all gather round. She'd have to open it in front of them and read out my poem, and they'd all laugh and tease her. So I gave the corner a flick that sent it deep into the dark heart of the locker.

And the second I did it, I understood everything, in a flash of intense white light. What I understood was this: giving a poem to Ari was the most stupid thing any human being had ever done in the history of the world. It was dumb, embarrassing, awkward, idiotic, cringe worthy, gormless, lame brained and shameful.

I had to get the card back.

Had to destroy it.

Not just bin it, but burn it. Or flush it. Or dissolve it in acid, the way murderers do with bodies.

I tried feeling around with my nail under the metal door. It was hopeless. The card was somewhere right at the back. I'd never get it unless I had some ... I don't know, wire or something.

I got an exercise book out of my bag. I opened it out flat, put the stiff cover under the door and slid it around, hoping to snag the card. I felt something, and hope rose in me for a second. Maybe the way the turtle felt a quick beat of hope when the fishermen took it from the net and before the long knife went in. But all I'd done was push the card even further back.

"What are you doing here?"

The words cut like that knife – the long, flexible, murderous knife of the turtle butchers. I felt it go under my shell.

I staggered back from the locker and saw the tracksuit of Mr Cudworth. Cudworth was an old-style PE teacher, as thick as mince and filled with the desire to inflict pain. Obviously, he wasn't allowed to batter the kids, like they could in the olden days. But if you offended him by being unsporty, for example, then you were in deep trouble. He'd order you to give him fifty press-ups or get you to climb the ropes dangling from the roof of the gym while everyone else watched. And the thing is that climbing a rope is pretty much impossible when you're unsporty. Some overweight kid, or some skinny runt, would try to crawl up the rope, with Cudworth yelling, "Move it, short arse!" or "Shift yourself, string bean!" at them. They'd get about six centimetres off the ground and that was it. Either they'd hang on the ropes, panting and terrified, or they'd drop to the wooden floor and squirm and grovel. Everyone would laugh, while Cudworth stood over them with his hairy arms on his hips, all happy for once because he'd got to inflict some pain and humiliation.

I lived in terror of being picked on by Cudworth and made to crawl up that damn rope in front of everyone. Luckily, my special skill came to my rescue in PE lessons: the skill of invisibility. I wasn't good enough or useless enough at sport to get noticed. I'd had PE lessons with Cudworth for four years, but he had no idea who I was.

That was fortunate, but my mind was still a blank as I stood in front of the locker.

"Well, boy?" Cudworth bellowed. "What are you doing?"

"Nothing," I replied.

Mistake. Cudworth hated it when you didn't call him sir.

"NOTHING WHAT?"

"Nothing, sir," I said.

I couldn't have said anything more guilty sounding than, "Nothing." It would have sounded better if I'd said, "Setting fire to the school, sir." It didn't help that what I'd said was actually, "N-n-n-nothing, sir," the stammering clearly showing my guilt.

Even someone as dumb as Cudworth knew that "n-n-n-nothing" really means "s-s-something". He started to come towards me in this sort of Neanderthal crouch, his arms and legs bent, that Cudworth always went into when he was trying to look athletic.

Then I realised I was holding the perfect excuse.

"Forgot my book, SIR!" I said, yelling the "sir" the way he liked it and holding out my Geography exercise book. I even let the pages flap open like a big white dog's tongue, revealing my notes and the drawings of ox-bow lakes and my charts showing banana production levels in Guatemala from 1994 to 2012.

Cudworth staggered to a stop. His hands grabbed and squeezed the air as if he were imagining wringing the neck of some small creature. He looked at the book, looked at my face, looked back at the book.

"Get lost," Cudworth said, and made a gesture with his thumb.

I didn't want to go to class. I'd be late, which would attract too much attention. Like I said, my skill was slipping under the radar. The door creaking open into the class, the faces turned my way, the teacher questioning me: these were the opposite of invisibility. If I didn't go to class, nobody would even know I hadn't been there.

Break was in half an hour. It was impossible to slip out of school now – there were CCTV cameras, and locked gates you had to get opened by speaking into an intercom to the office.

But I knew a good place to go. Behind the school kitchens there was a separate building with the school boiler in it, nothing much more than a brick box the size of a garage. The door was at the bottom of some steps, well below ground level. The door was always locked, but the space outside the door was invisible from the rest of the school. I made my way to the boiler building and crouched in the shadows, grinding my teeth and wringing my hands as I thought about the dumb thing I'd done.

Chapter 7
The Bike

I almost fell asleep down there outside the boiler room in the dark. I went into the stupor you get just before sleep, a place in between waking and dreaming. I must have been tired – I don't suppose I'd had much sleep the night before, what with Mum, and thinking up the stupid poem, and imagining what Ari would think of it. But the stupor was nice. I was thinking of Ari, imagining her face as she read my poem, and for once the dream didn't end in horror.

I was pulled out of it by the sounds of break: the bell, kids screaming and laughing, feet pounding.

I looked up and saw faces staring back down at me – some skulking Year 10s. They were about as tough as it got in our school, though in most other schools they'd have been lightweights.

"Get out of it, weirdo," said a kid with a buzz cut and one eyebrow. It was always a relief, being called something like weirdo or jerk rather than you-know-what.

I squeezed past the Year 10s and walked back around to the front of the school. I was heading for the library, where I normally hid out at break and lunch. It meant going past the bike shed – not really a shed, just a long line of steel racks covered by a grey plastic roof.

And she was there.

You always know when the person you love is near. If you don't get that, don't understand what I mean, then you've never been in love. You feel the special energy of them, pulsing and flickering like a broken strip light, except it's glorious and not irritating.

Ari was with the golden gang. Plus a few extra kids. They were laughing and mucking about. I knew Ari cycled in to school. Of course I did. I knew everything about her that you could know from far away and nothing that you could know from close up.

It was obvious what was going on. Ari had a
new bike. A birthday bike. Her old one was pretty
beaten up, and this new bike was a beauty. I even
recognised the make and the model. I'd always
dreamed of having a bike, and I used to look at ads
and reviews on the internet, so bikes were a thing I
knew about.

It was midnight-black and stripped down –
lean, mean, kind of evil looking. Everything about
it was essential. I mean, there was nothing that
didn't need to be there, no frills, no flash, no waste.
The coolest thing about the bike was the fork –
normally two joined prongs at the front of the bike
where the wheel fits. But this bike didn't have
two forks, only one. It's called a "lefty", meaning
that the single fork connects on the left side of the
wheel. It looked wrong and right, so right, at the
same time.

"That is so bad-ass!" said Ez, and did a sort of
twisting dance of pleasure.

"She's beautiful," sighed Si, and you knew he
meant the bike but also kind of Ari.

Ari wasn't usually a goofy grinner. She did
small perfect smiles, smiles that were like a bird
flying past the window, vanishing before you really
saw them. But now she had this great beaming

smile that made it seem like the sun was shining even though the sky was the colour of a dead whale.

"It's from my dad," Ari was saying. "He had to …" But then her voice petered out. The golden gang didn't notice – they were too busy cooing and caressing the bike. But it was an odd sort of thing to say, and I found myself wondering what was going to come next. "He had to … get it shipped in specially from America"? "He had to … pay £1,000 extra for the slick paint job"?

No, it wasn't like that. What Ari had been about to say was something else. Something harder. Like "… work extra shifts" or "… save up for a year". But the parents of the golden kids didn't have to save up or work extra shifts in Tesco or Pizza Hut.

I was chewing over these thoughts, and also just enjoying the scene and the happiness of Ari, when I got a tingly back-of-the-neck feeling. A second later I realised that Moll was looking at me. She was the one whose face was always doing stuff – always in motion, laughing, smiling, grimacing or whatever. But now she was just looking, her face still, silent. Like she'd been Botoxed to death.

This was bad.

And then she nudged Si with her elbow. He looked down at her (you had to look down at Moll because she was tiny, like some kind of pixie or elf), and she nodded towards me. So then two of them were looking at me.

I turned away and walked quickly towards the main doors, almost scampering. And even as this was happening, I knew that running away was the worst thing I could do. It screamed out, "I'VE BEEN STARING AT ARI BECAUSE I'M SO IN LOVE WITH HER I CAN'T STOP MYSELF."

If I'd wandered slowly away, it would have been so much better – or even just stood there like I was staring into space, into nothing. But my cheeks were already blushing a red so deep it looked … Well, I don't know what it looked like because I was on the inside of it, but it felt like my whole head was going to blow the hell up, and there was a rushing, echoey sound in my ears, like when you listen to the sea in a seashell.

I reached the library and wormed my way between the stacks until I was in my favourite quiet corner at the back where there was a chair I loved. It wasn't even a special chair, just a chair, but it was mine. I sat and put my head in my hands and waited for the bell to go, like the Minotaur, safely back at the heart of his labyrinth. And I didn't even think about lunch, although it was school lunches that pretty much kept me alive.

Chapter 8

An Eagle – a Kestrel

Luckily I didn't have lessons with Ari or any of the golden gang that afternoon. So I just sat through Geography and then through Maths gazing out of the window at the grey skies. I got to know those clouds pretty well. They weren't the cheerful fluffy clouds with blue in between, but the kind where the solid grey thickens and folds and rumples, like the blankets on an unmade bed.

It wasn't so much being caught staring that was eating me but the poem. My soul was just shrivelling at the thought of it. It was as embarrassing as my mum's mobility scooter. I was terrified that somehow Ari would trace it back to me. I played out the scene in my head a hundred times, each with a small variation. It was like some torturer from the olden times who knew you couldn't just inflict the same torments day after day but had to vary it – one session pulling out the nails, the next whipping the soles of your feet with a bamboo cane, the next taking out your eye with a spoon.

The ache in my guts from hunger after skipping lunch also didn't help much.

I went to the library again after the bell for the end of school. The librarian, Mrs Sunda, let kids hang around for half an hour. The other library kids were mainly helpless Year 7 and 8s, and a few other bookish older kids. They all had little blue and gold badges with "Library Monitor" written on them. They liked to be given jobs by Mrs Sunda, stacking and stamping and sorting the stationery cupboard, or drawing pictures of characters from books to pin up on the art board.

I didn't get involved with any of that stuff. I just sat in my favourite chair and read, waiting for the world outside to quieten down, and killing time so I didn't have to spend all my life sitting in the flat with Mum.

There was a Year 8 kid called … well, I didn't really know his name. Cuthbert, maybe. Something like that. One of those names you should only give your kids if you hate them and want them to have a crap time at school. This Cuthbert, or maybe Clarence, had these round glasses on his round face on top of his round body, and if you looked at his eyes, they looked like little fish swimming in a bowl. So he came up to me while I sat in my chair. I was looking at the pages of my book, but the words were just shapes without meaning, as if I'd never learned to read. Cuthbert said, "Mrs Sunda says will you help me take down the art from the top of the art board, because I can't reach it."

"Stand on a chair," I said without looking up.

Cuthbert half turned away, and then he spun back and said, "Standing on chairs is health and safety."

"What?" I said.

"Standing on chairs is a health and safety issue. Do you want a sweet?"

And then Cuthbert dug down in his trouser pocket and rooted around in there. After a while he pulled out this bag of Haribo Star Mix, and you could see they'd sort of melded together from the heat and the pressure, like the way the heat in a volcano melts the rocks together. But the weird thing was that I was so hungry, my mouth started to juice up, and I really, really wanted a sweet.

I looked at Cuthbert, with his round everything, and his eyes still moving like fish in the bowl of his head. And without meaning to, I said, "Yeah," and I put out my hand to this Year 8 dweeb. At least he didn't put his own moist paw into the bag and get a sweet out for me. He sort of squeezed out one, two, three, by running his fat fingers up the outside of the bag.

And next thing I knew I was following Cuthbert, or Cecil, or Colin, or whatever his name was, to the big board with the art. Mrs Sunda was doing librarian stuff behind her desk.

"Good to see you helping out, Matthew," she said, even though I hadn't done anything yet.

I shrugged at her in a cool way.

"Read anything good lately?" she asked me.

It was Mrs Sunda who had suggested *Watership Down* all those years ago, the book about the rabbits.

I shrugged, and didn't mean to get involved in a discussion. Some kids are good at talking to the teachers. They're the kind of kids who have conversations with their parents about politics and the news and I don't know what. I couldn't talk to teachers, couldn't look into their faces without stammering or blushing or just having a big nothing in my head. But all by itself, my mouth started to talk.

"I've just read a book about the Romans, Miss. The Ninth Legion disappeared in Scotland, and this Roman officer goes to find out what happened. His dad was in the lost legion. That's why he was so bothered. And he wanted to get the Eagle back, which is sort of the emblem of the legion."

Mrs Sunda smiled and nodded. She had a nice face. There was grey in her hair.

"You liked it?" she asked.

"It was a bit complicated," I said. "Slow at the beginning. But exciting at the end."

"So what next?"

I shrugged again.

Mrs Sunda got up from behind her desk and disappeared into the shelves. I helped the round kid with the art, getting my nail under the drawing pins. The art was mostly rubbish. They'd gone over the lines, like babies. If you're going to colour stuff in, you should do it properly.

"Try this one," said Mrs Sunda.

I looked at the title. *A Kestrel for a Knave?*

"Is it about a bird?" I asked.

"It has a bird in it. But it's more about the people. About a boy."

"It's thin," I said, not knowing what else to say about the book.

"Thin but deep," Mrs Sunda said, smiling again.

I gave her my third shrug. It was a shrug that said, "OK." I carried the book back to my chair, put it in my bag and slipped out.

Chapter 9
Stolen!

I began walking home. The crowd of kids outside the school had thinned to a few stragglers blown along the street like leaves. There was a cafe a few streets from the school. I always got a little surge of feelings when I walked past it, because sometimes the golden gang were in there. I could have gone home a different way, but just getting a glimpse of Ari as I walked by always gave me a glow that lasted until I got home to Mum.

I was still a hundred metres away from the cafe when I saw them all burst out, like pop from a shaken bottle – Ari, Si, Moll, Ez. The A-Team. They were doing their usual thing, turning themselves into a kind of joint animal, like coral or whatever – being different things and one thing all at the same time. Their arms were around each other, their many heads thrown back together in laughter.

I stepped back into a shop doorway. No special reason why. I just didn't want Ari seeing me alone in the street. Lonely. Loser. Lonely loser.

As I watched, I saw first Ari and then the others change. They were standing near some railings outside a boring office building. There was nothing there. But the nothing was obviously a *bad* nothing. Ari put her head in her hands. Si's face was all concern, mixed up with anger. Ez used the bad words, all of them.

And then I worked it out.

It was her bike, her new bike.

It had been there.

Now it wasn't.

I really felt this. Most of the problems of the golden gang weren't my problems. The problem of which brand of jeans to get. The problem of where to go on holiday: Florida or Barbados. But this was something I could understand. A new bike, stolen. I felt the pang of it, almost as if it'd been my bike.

Grief and anger make you ugly. It's one of those universal things. Ari's perfect appearance was broken, ruined. Her face lost its unity and harmony, and became many different things all at once, as if six different faces had been crammed together. It twisted and scrunched and then became blank. It cracked up into broken slabs and then melted together again, like Cuthbert's Haribos.

And I suppose you know when you have these special feelings for someone, because they don't disappear when you see a face made ugly by pain, they get stronger. I felt a new thing now, something deeper than what had been in my heart before.

I felt sorrow and sympathy for Ari. Before, my love had been as light as helium, lifting me up the way you see a tiny kid with a balloon and you think the balloon will lift them into the air and carry them away. But now my love weighed heavy in me, as if I were carrying someone dead in my arms.

I heard some of the things the golden gang were saying as they drifted on the wind.

"Insurance will cover it."

"I'll call the police."

"No point. They never ..."

It went on for a while, and gradually Ari got her face back under control. And then, one by one, the others wandered away, saying their last goodbyes. That seemed wrong to me. They should have stayed with her. The last to leave was Moll. She hugged Ari, and as she did she looked over Ari's shoulder and right into my eyes. I glanced away, trying hard this time to look casual. But still, Moll's face went a bit odd, puzzled, suspicious.

Then she was gone, and Ari was waiting alone at the bus stop.

It was then that I made the decision. I was going to go and talk to her. I began walking towards the bus stop, practising what I was going to say: "I heard about your bike. I'm really sorry. I'm Stinky Mog, I look like a tramp and I smell like a bog."

Of course I wasn't going to talk to her.

I stopped dead in the street, looking down at myself. My trousers were too short. My jumper had holes in the sleeves. My coat was from Oxfam. The nylon shell had split and you could see the foam stuff on the inside. My hands had the not-quite-clean look you get when you wash them in cold water without soap. My hair was lank and greasy.

I was never going to talk to Ari. Ever.

She waited there for the bus, sitting on the little metal shelf in the bus shelter, and I saw her put her hand in her bag and draw out an envelope.

I realised then that the saying "go weak at the knees" is actually true. I felt suddenly like my legs were made of jelly.

And then, with Ari still holding the envelope, the bus came.

I had no control over what happened next. I saw Ari get on. Then I joined the bulging queue, flashed my pass and walked to the back of the bus. I strolled right past Ari, who was sitting near the front. She didn't look up at me, and if she had, so what? She didn't know I lived in the opposite direction. I could just have been going home.

It was insane, I know, but I just needed to see Ari reading my poem. Needed to see her face. Needed to find out if she laughed scornfully and scrunched it up, or smiled and folded it to her heart.

The bus was full. I got the last seat at the back. I had to try to snatch glances of Ari in between the women with bags of shopping, workmen in hi-vis jackets and scabby schoolkids.

But then Ari turned to gaze out of the window, and I got a clear look at her face, or the side of it, at least. Her expression was calmer now, but I saw tears streaming down her cheek. For a moment I thought that maybe it was the poem that had made her cry. I imagined going up to her and telling her it was from me, and she'd look at me with wonder and amazement, and then everything would be possible. But then I saw that Ari was still holding the unopened envelope, and I knew she was crying about her bike.

The bus chugged through town. I thought she'd live on one of the posh streets, but we went past them. Soon we were in a boring bit of town – not edgy, like where I live, but just sort of nothing streets with pound shops and other shops with "Vacant" signs on them. So then I thought Ari probably lived in one of the posh suburbs, much further from here. That would be a long bike ride ... But suddenly she got up. The bus stopped and Ari got off, here in the nothing streets, with poor, boring houses.

And of course then I understood. Understood about the bike. Understood why it was a tragedy for the bike to be stolen. She wasn't like the other golden kids. Ari was poor. Not poor like me, but just normal poor. The poor of ordinary people doing normal jobs for only just enough money. Money they couldn't afford to waste on stolen bikes.

I got off the bus at the next stop. I didn't see which way Ari went, and I wouldn't have followed her anyway. I wasn't a stalker.

I walked back home. It took me more than an hour. And as I walked, I worked out a plan. It was a good plan. If it worked, then everything would be different. I would make Ari happy. It was Friday. My plan was for Monday. I had three days to make Ari smile.

Chapter 10

The Plan, and Laughter

I knew what would happen with Ari's bike. The bike gangs steal bikes. In the olden days they'd take them down to the market to flog. Now they use eBay or Facebook or Gumtree. And they want a fast turnover, so they put them up for sale as soon as they can and sell them dirt cheap. Same day, next day.

All I had to do was find the bike, go and meet the thieves, ask for a test ride, then cycle off as fast as Stinky Mog's legs would go. Simples.

Back home, Mum seemed a bit better than she had been for a while. Her hair was brushed and she had proper clothes on. Her child benefit money was in, so I went to the shops and bought some tuna and pasta and sweetcorn and tomatoes and mixed them up together to make a salad. It's an easy thing to make, even for a fool like Stinky Mog. And I was famished, as I'd eaten nothing all day.

I bolted it down, made sure Mum was OK in front of the telly and told her I was going out.

"Where are you off to, love?" Mum asked, which showed she was in a better place. Sometimes she wouldn't even know when I was in or out.

"Library. Homework."

And I was going to the library, so it wasn't a lie.

It was a good library. It was still open late two evenings a week, despite the government cuts. I had a library card, but I also sometimes bought the battered old books they had on sale for 10p. But today I wasn't after the books. I went straight to the computers and got to work. I checked all the sites, searching for the make and model of Ari's bike.

There were a few hits, but not the right one. Some of the bikes for sale were too far away. Some were the wrong size or too old. I'd got excited about the plan, too excited. It was too soon for the bike to be put up for sale, even for the gangs.

I got back home at half eight. Mum was snoozing in front of the telly. I brought her a cup of tea and some biscuits, and she woke up.

And then we had a conversation. It was something that hadn't happened in a long time. I mean, we talked sometimes – a few words here and there while watching the telly – but this was different.

"I went to the doctor today," Mum said. "There's a new one there. She's young. A kid, really."

"Are you sick, Mum?" I asked.

"It wasn't that. Well, it was, sort of."

"What do you mean?"

"I haven't been … good," Mum said. "Not for a long time. I know that."

I just sat there and sipped my tea. I didn't know what to say.

"The thing is, the things that were wrong with me … well, Dr Harrison gave me pills for it. And the pills helped a bit. Helped with what was wrong with me. But then the pills became what was wrong with me. You get to need them, even when the thing you first needed them for isn't there any more, if you follow what I mean. Wait, let me turn this off."

That was a shock. The telly was always on. We never talked without it humming away in the background. The remote was bust, so you had to turn it off and on using a button on the front. Mum tried to get up, rocking a few times to get the momentum to stand, but then I just went and turned it off for her.

I looked at Mum, and I could see she seemed a bit different. It wasn't just that she'd run the brush through her hair or put on fresh clothes. It was her face. It wasn't as dead as it had been.

"And this doctor – did I say she was an Indian lady?" Mum went on. "Well, we had a talk. Dr Harrison never had the time to talk. I just got my prescription off him. That was all he was good for. But this new one, she talked. And she asked me things. Things about my life. And about you. Because I know ... I know I haven't been ... but I'm trying to be better. The lady doctor, she said I can't just come off the pills, because I'll go mental with it. Not that she said mental of course. But she's lowered the strength of the pills. And then she gave me some other pills to help with coming off the first lot, which seems a bit daft but sort of makes sense. And already I feel like I'm waking up a bit. A bit more my old self."

Then I asked her something. Something I'd never really thought about before.

"How old are you, Mum?"

And she laughed. It was a funny sound – I mean funny weird, not funny funny. It was as if Mum was using something for the first time ever. Like she'd found some musical instrument in the street and just decided to blow it to see what happened.

"I'm forty-two," she said.

I didn't know what to think then. Obviously, when you're a teenager, forty-two is ancient, older than you can imagine, like from the time of the dinosaurs. But also not that old. And with my mum being in the mess she was, weirdly I thought of her as older even than that – as *old* old.

"And the lady doctor," Mum continued, "said that it's going to be difficult coming off the pills after all these years, even with the other pills to help. She said I'd need therapy – talking therapy to help with it. So I've got an appointment to see someone."

"A shrink?" I said in a sort of American accent. I don't know why. Just a kind of joke. And Mum smiled again, and I realised it was probably the first joke we'd ever shared together.

"Yeah, a shrink. Someone to talk to. A therapist, that's the word. But the doctor said that

I'm going to be hard to live with while this is going on. Shouty and that."

"I don't mind, Mum."

"And I won't be much use round the house. Looking after you sort of thing."

I don't know if she'd said it as a joke, or just realised how funny it was – funny in a tragic sort of way, because she'd never looked after me – but we both started laughing, and this time she got the hang of it. Soon our flat was filled with a sound it had never known before: two people laughing in that gloomy, messy, dirty, sad, lonely place.

Chapter 11

A Bite

The public library opened at ten on Saturday morning. I arrived right as the librarian unlocked the door so I could make sure I got one of the computers. You were only supposed to book them for an hour at a time, but I told the librarian I needed it all day for a project for my GCSEs. I put so much longing and desperation into my act that even I believed my fibs.

So I set up camp on the computer and kept circling through the sites – Facebook and eBay and Gumtree – waiting for Ari's bike to pop up. I was so sure it would appear that I wasn't even nervous about it. I was like some nut from a religious cult who knows, just knows, that a spaceship is going to come down from heaven and pick them up and take them to paradise.

Eleven o'clock came. And then twelve. I really did have some homework, so I did that to fill in the time until the bike appeared. At two I was hungry. I had just enough money to get some chips. I sat and ate them in the churchyard, sitting on a bench. Normally I'd enjoy every one, savouring the first chips that were so hot they burnt your mouth, right down to the last ones, soggy with vinegar. But I just scoffed them as fast as I could, which was a waste of my last pound.

Back in the library I had to wait half an hour for a computer to come free, and it was the longest half hour of my life. I wandered around the shelves, but all I could think about was Ari and the bike and how I'd get it back. I worked out all the details, thought through what might go wrong and how to deal with it.

When I was back in front of the computer, I was convinced that the bike would be right there, waiting for me.

Nothing.

Nothing on eBay, nothing on Gumtree, nothing on Facebook.

I began to think that maybe the bike was so sweet that whoever nicked it wanted it for themselves. But that was crazy. No one would keep a stolen bike like that around here. It would stand out too much.

The people in the library began to thin out. It closed at six. It wasn't open on Sunday. I was going to fail.

"Homework all done?" someone asked.

It was the librarian. He was a young guy. Thought he was cool, I suppose. Little beard, skinny jeans.

I shrugged.

"You can print out your work, you know," the guy added.

"Costs too much," I said. It did. It was 20p a sheet.

"So what were you doing?" he asked.

"Just researching."

"OK, well, if you need anything."

"Yeah. Thanks," I said.

He looked at his watch.

"We close in twenty—"

"Yeah, I know."

Then he went off and tried to make friends with some other kids.

At five minutes to six, I gave up. I told myself it didn't matter, that I hadn't lost anything. But I'd imagined myself proudly wheeling the bike up to Ari on Monday morning, just smiling, letting her see what I'd done, letting her work it out. And those images now crumbled away. It was all stupid.

I went through the sites one last time: eBay, Gumtree, Facebook.

And there it was. Beautiful.

In my town.

The pic wasn't a photo of the actual bike – it was just a pic pulled off a website. Clever. The actual photo would have been too much of a giveaway, too much of an admission of guilt.

"*Get this Bad Boy,*" the advert read. "*Top notch. Clean. Good tires. £300. No offs.*"

£300. The bike must have cost a grand to buy brand new.

"Closing up now," said a voice behind me.

"Five minutes," I pleaded without looking round.

"Just be quick."

I wrote a reply. I had to give myself a name. I thought for a couple of seconds and decided: Minotaur.

"*Want this. Will pay cash. Meet anytime.*"

But the words felt wrong, so I didn't hit send. It sounded too desperate.

"*Cool bike. Need for uni. Free tomorrow?*"

These bike gangs all hate students but think they are easy pickings. No one is worried about a student getting tough.

I sent the message. I was the last person left in the library. Unless we arranged a meeting before I went, I was sunk.

"*Yeh ok,*" the reply came through. "*U wont b sorry. Meet in the carpark in Brooke Towers. You know it?*"

"*I'll find it. What time?*" I typed.

"*Busy in day tomorrow. Say 6 evening?*"

"*Perfect. See you then. Don't sell it to anyone else.*"

"*My word is my word. Bring cash.*"

"*See you.*"

"*Yeh.*"

I'd been holding my breath, but now it came out as a huge sigh.

"You finished, young man?"

The librarian had been waiting patiently for me. He was OK.

"Yeah, thanks," I said.

"Have a good one."

Chapter 12

The Heist

The next day was heaven and hell all jumbled up together. The heaven was when I imagined Ari's face turning from despair to joy.

The hell was imagining it all going wrong.

And there were so many ways it could go wrong.

I knew Brooke Towers.

It was dangerous.

Where I lived was a dump, but Brooke Towers took it to the next level. It was gangland. Worse than that, it was the no man's land that different gangs fought over. Dangerous for outsiders. Heck, dangerous for insiders.

I didn't have any spare thoughts left over for Mum. She went out for a bit. I asked if she needed my help to get down to her mobility scooter, but she said she'd do it. I should have asked where she was going, but I didn't care. Today I only had room in my head for one thing.

At five I started to get everything prepared. I had an old backpack with a broken strap. It looked like the kind of thing you'd carry your laptop around in. I filled it full of random crap from the flat. A couple of old magazines, the broken remote, a small frying pan without a handle and with the non-stick stuff all worn away. The backpack felt like it could easily contain a laptop and other student stuff.

I looked at myself in the mirror. I didn't look much like a student. I tried combing my hair in different ways. No good. I just looked like a grotty schoolkid. I looked in the drawer where we kept hats and gloves and found an old hat of my mum's. Just a plain woollen hat. Kind of an old-lady hat, but on me it looked like the sort of thing a student might wear. And then I had a brainwave. My mum had a shabby winter coat, older than me. I tried it on. It was big and shapeless and sort of brown. It was perfect. I really did look a bit like a student who was trying to be alternative.

Brooke Towers was a half-hour walk away. It was already dark by the time I set off, thank god –

I didn't want anyone to see me in my mad student outfit. And darkness would be my friend when I got there.

There were four blocks that made up Brooke Towers, almost like the guard towers of some old castle. Each one was thirteen storeys high. From a distance, they looked pretty impressive. Get close and you could see what a mess they were in, with broken windows, and graffiti on every reachable bit of wall.

In the middle there was the children's playground, with broken swings and broken roundabouts and a climbing frame where hard kids hung out looking for smaller kids to mug. And next to the playground, the car park. As I approached, it was empty apart from a single burnt-out car and a skip with bits of broken furniture sticking out.

The whole scene was lit by this sickly orange glow from the street lights. It looked like some old painting of hell. You could only imagine bad things happening here. Torture and torment and murder.

And so part of me was relieved that no one was there. Once they saw me they might see through me and my outfit and leave me bleeding.

I stood on the edge of the car park for a couple of minutes. It was quarter past six. I felt creeped out. It didn't help that I felt more than a bit conspicuous in Mum's old hat and coat.

Time to split.

Except I had a feeling I was being watched.

I reached into the backpack and pulled out the broken TV remote. I pretended to call someone on it, then to send a text. Of course from a few metres away it would be obvious that it wasn't no iPhone, but in the dark, from a distance ... maybe it would look legit. I slipped the "phone" back in the bag with the magazines and broken frying pan.

And then shapes began to emerge from the shadows. One, two, three. One short, one lanky and one big and solid. You could imagine a car smashing into the last one and him just walking on, maybe breaking his stride, but nothing more, while the car was a write-off.

In my years of being picked on, I'd learned a few things. One is that you never know who the really mean kid is going to be. Sometimes it's the little one, but you can't rely on that, because sometimes it's the big one. But there's another rule: a big mean one is worse than a little mean one. And you also can't assume the little one is the brains and the big one is the muscle. You get little thick kids and big brainy ones. So all I'm saying is that misery gets delivered in all kinds of packages.

The lanky kid was wheeling a bike.

Ari's bike.

But not quite. They'd changed the saddle, and the handlebar grips were a different colour – a nasty yellow rather than the cool black. I'd heard they do that, the thieves, to disguise the bikes in case the police turn up with a description. Something like that, anyway. Not that the police ever bother with bikes. Not round here.

I had an almost uncontrollable urge to run. All the years of horror at school had been different to this. I'd never really felt afraid. I'd felt ashamed, not afraid. And you can't run away from shame. Shame sticks to you.

There's something I read in a book once. It was about the difference between shame and guilt. You feel guilty for something you've done, some bad thing. And because it's something you've done, there's a way out. You can make it better, or you can say sorry. You can promise not to do it again.

But shame isn't about what you've done – it's about what you are. And so nothing wipes it clean.

"You Minotaur?" said the big kid. He had a high voice, which was almost funny.

I hesitated, forgetting the name I'd given myself. Then I was back on it.

"Yeah," I replied.

I tried to make my voice sound deeper and gave myself an accent from out of town.

I looked at the bike. Even in the orange light of the car park you could see how sleek and beautiful it was.

"You got coin?" That was the short kid.

I tapped my pocket. Would they ask to see it? There was still time to run. They wouldn't bother chasing me if I just ran off now. Why would they? They'd just think I was a chicken-shit student, out of his depth.

"Tell you what, man," said Big, in his high voice. "We call it two-eighty, and you keep twenty and buy yourself a new coat."

The others burst out laughing. But this was all good. This was almost laughing with me, not at me. Almost.

"I need a test ride," I said. "Make sure it's all OK."

"The bike's good, solid." Lanky lifted up the front of the bike and let it bounce down on the front tyre.

"I can see," I said. "It's sweet. Just gotta test it for size."

I slipped the backpack off my shoulder.

"You look after this," I said casually. "Got my laptop and phone in it."

I held the backpack out and Big took it, felt the heft of it. He grunted. I knew then that I was OK, that it was going to work. As far as they were concerned, they had my laptop and phone, so I wasn't going to split.

"Stay in the quad," said Shorty.

"Course."

I took the bike from Lanky.

Sometimes you want something to feel heavy in your hands and sometimes you want it to be light. This bike was so light I could have held it up with two fingers. I climbed on. Ari was tall for a girl, but the saddle was still a bit low for me.

Didn't matter.

I cycled slowly for a few metres, turned and began to cycle back. I was eyeing up my escape route, plotting a course to safety. I should have done this before I got on the bike, but stress and fear can blunt you, make your thoughts slow and clumsy.

I was also remembering how to ride. I was no real cyclist, but I'd had enough goes on the bikes of neighbourhood kids when I was little to learn how to do it. And, yeah, it came back to me. But smooth I wasn't.

"You want stabilisers?" yelled Big, and the other two laughed again. They were enjoying themselves. That was good. They were even more at ease.

It looked like the best way was out through one corner of the quad, then left down one street, right down another, and then I'd hit the high street and safety. I mean, they could hardly run along there yelling out, "Oi, bring back that bike we stole!"

"Nice, eh?" called out Big.

It was time.

I turned the bike away again, just going slow, weaving from side to side, acting like I was checking out the steering. And it was frisky – I mean the lightest touch sent the bike one way, and when you tried to correct it you went too far the other. I paused and balanced on the pedals, keeping the bike almost completely still. There was a moment of silence, when the darkness beat in my ears, and then I was off, full speed, heading for the corner.

It took maybe three seconds for the bike gang to realise what was going on. Then I heard a shout, a yell, a curse. I glanced back. Big was emptying the crap out of my rucksack. Then they were after me, running. Shorty was fastest away, but soon Lanky overtook him, with Big lumbering at the back. They had no chance. No way could they catch me, not when I had the head start. Over five metres a running kid can beat a bike, but after that, no contest!

And then I did it. It was the most Unstinky Mog thing I'd ever done. I took one hand off the handlebars, twisted round and gave them the finger. And it was a slow one, done with feeling. I was giving the finger to all the tormentors. It was a finger to history.

It was also dumb. The bike was so fidgety and flighty, and, like I said, I was a rubbish cyclist. I went into a serious wobble. I thought I was going down. But I just managed to pull the bike out of the spin, and I was OK and away.

Still, the wobble gave Lanky, Shorty and Big encouragement, and they yelled again and sped up, thinking they could catch me. They were wrong, and part of me was glad that they were still trying. It would have been too easy otherwise. I wanted them to feel the hope now so they could feel the despair later.

I reached the corner of the quad and hit the first of the dark streets beyond, my heart singing with joy and excitement.

But I had to focus. I was still in a stupidly low gear, so my legs were a blur without me hitting anywhere near top speed. The gears were complicated, with shifters on the left and right side. I thumbed the one on my left.

Another mistake.

It was for the front derailleur, not the rear – for the three big cogs attached to the pedals. And I'd clicked it too far. Or maybe, as it was a new bike, the gears weren't set up quite right. Either way, same result. The chain came off the inside cog, and suddenly my legs were spinning on air and the bike was slowing.

No!

No!

No!

Now I had to decide. I could get off the bike and run it to the high street, then try to lose myself in the crowds. Or I could stop dead and try to slip the chain back on the cog. If I did it in time, I'd be away again. If I didn't, and they caught me, they'd stamp my face into the gutter. And why would they just beat me to a pulp? Why stop there? I'd made them look stupid. I'd given them the finger. That was the dumbest thing Stinky Mog ever did. Why not kill me, teach a lesson to the world? You messed with the Brooke Towers boys at your peril.

Screw it.

I got off the bike as it was still rolling. I half stumbled but managed to stay on my feet. It was too dark to see where I was going properly. There was a street light a few metres further down the street. I sprinted to it with the bike. I bent over the front derailleur, got my fingers down there. The chain was rammed in close to the frame. My fingers shook, fumbled. I heard another shout. The boys had emerged from the quad. They were maybe thirty seconds away. But I didn't look, no time. I got my fingers under the chain, wrenched it up to the teeth of the cog, trapped my fingers between the cog and the chain. I pulled them free, but that slipped the chain back off the cog. Panic. Terror. This wasn't the old fear of Stinky Mog. This was a new fear. The fear of the hunted.

Again I caught the chain, again pulled it on to the cog. This time I got my fingers out of the way. Now I could hear their trainers slapping on the pavement, hear their eager panting breath. Still I didn't look. I ran with the bike, getting some speed up. Jumped on it, smooth for once in my life. Pushed the pedals, felt the chain bite. More terror – would the chain slip off again? But it was good. It was good. It was good.

I heard a change in the breath of the chasers. Heard the defeat in their panting. But I wasn't looking back. I built my speed. Just as I turned left, I saw a kid walking towards the towers – not one of the chasers but a new one. He looked at me, saw my face. There was a flash of recognition. And then it came out of his mouth just as I was halfway along that road and getting ready to turn right into the safety of the high street.

I heard his voice shout:

Stinky Mog
Stinky Mog
He looks like a ...

The song trailed off as I left him behind and headed for home.

Chapter 13

Not Sad

I left the bike in the downstairs hall, next to Mum's mobility scooter. The cool and uncool side by side. Like me standing next to Ari ...

I felt ... well, I didn't have the words for it. Excited. Triumphant. Scared. Alive. I'd never done anything like this. And normally that wouldn't be a big deal. There were lots of things I hadn't done that normal people did all the time. I'd never been to the cinema. I'd never had a holiday. I'd never had a phone. But now I'd done something that was ... AMAZING! Maybe even completely bloody unique. I'd stolen back a bike from a gang of thieves. Maybe nobody had ever done that before.

I wanted to tell Mum about it, but of course I couldn't. It just isn't the sort of thing you tell your parents, even normal ones.

And, anyway, Mum was in a foul mood. She wasn't normally bothered about where I was, but now she gave me a right earful.

"Where have you been?" Mum asked.

"Out," I replied.

"Out where?"

"Just out."

"Out where?"

"Library."

"On a Sunday? I don't think so."

"I forgot it was closed. So then I went to a ... friend's."

"What friend?"

"Just a friend."

She paused then. Maybe she knew I didn't have any friends and that made her feel guilty.

"Have you done your homework?" Mum asked.

"Yeah," I said.

"Show me."

So I went and got my homework. She even looked at it.

"I made dinner," Mum said.

That was a shocker.

"What?"

"Dinner. Mashed potatoes and sausages. I waited, but you weren't here. Yours is in the oven."

And so that was the most normal evening I'd had in my entire life. Being nagged by my mum, eating a burnt dinner made for me by my mum. It doesn't take a lot to make a kid happy. No, that's not right. What I mean is that it doesn't take a lot to make a kid not sad. And so, for the first time I could ever remember, I wasn't sad.

Chapter 14

High and Low

I didn't know whether to walk Ari's bike into school or ride it there. Cycling it seemed somehow wrong, disrespectful, so I began by walking along beside it. But it was a bit awkward and annoying and it was taking me too long, so I hopped on the bike. It was such a joy to ride, smooth and sleek and fast, especially now I wasn't worried about being dragged off it and beaten to death in the street.

I tried again to imagine the scene as I gave it back to Ari. Her puzzled expression would turn first into a smile and then widen into a joyful laugh. The rest of the golden gang would be standing around with their mouths open. But then they'd smile too, and Si would slap me on the back, and Ez would try to be too funny, as usual. Moll would pull one of her exaggerated faces, like an actor asked to show "surprise" at an audition.

I had a little half smile on my face when I reached the school gates, thinking about all this.

And you know that what comes next isn't going to be good, don't you? You know that things won't be OK for Stinky Mog, because the world is meant for the golden ones and not for the kids like him.

I wove down the school drive from the gates towards the bike racks. It wasn't late, but it wasn't early, either, and kids were streaming in to their form classes, ready for morning registration. My plan was to park the bike and then wait till morning break to tell Ari, to lead her by the ... no, not by the hand, not yet. I'd say something like, "Hey, Ari, can I show you something?"

No, not that. That sounded weird and lame at the same time. Something. I'd think of something.

I got off the bike and leant it against the metal tube of the bike rack. And then it struck me that I didn't have anything to lock it up with. Some kids locked their bikes at school, others didn't bother. But most of the unlocked bikes were crap, and this was a beauty.

I was standing there thinking it through when I sensed something behind me – an onrushing energy, a noise. And then I felt a great shove in my back, and I was staggering forwards, out of control, falling, falling. Then I was flat on my face, my hands stinging with the slap of the concrete.

I didn't understand. Had some kid crashed his bike into me? For a mad second I thought that the Brooke Towers gang had tracked me down. And then I heard a familiar voice, but one twisted into an angry sneer.

"Thief. Caught you."

Still on the concrete floor, I turned. It was Si, out of breath as if he'd been running. And then the others joined him. First Ez. Then Moll. Then, last, Ari. Other random kids had noticed the scuffle and began to gather, too.

I tried to stand up, but Si stepped towards me and kicked me down again – not hard, not a brutal kick, more just a push with his foot.

"What's going on?" said Ari, looking from Si to me and back.

"Saw this jerk wheeling it in here," Si said.

"Wheeling what?" Ari asked.

"The bike, Ari. Look at it. It's yours!"

Ari looked. Her face was unreadable.

"He's changed the saddle and the handgrips," Si went on, "but it's your bike."

"I saw him staring the other day," said Moll. "Right here. And then he was hanging around after the cafe, when your bike was nicked."

"Who is this loser anyway?" said Si. "I don't even know who he is."

I'd been in classes with him for four years.

"Course you do," said Ez. "He's the nothing kid at the back."

"I still don't understand," said Ari. "What's happening?"

"I can't get over the cheek of it," said Si. "This kid, he steals your bike on Friday, changes the saddle and the grips and rides it in on Monday. Not only is he a THIEF" – he spat the word at me, hatred in his voice – "but he's thick as well."

Ari now spoke to me for the first time ever. I was still squirming on the floor.

"Is this true?" And then before I answered Ari added, "I know your name. Matthew."

"N-No," I stammered. "I didn't steal it!"

"So," Ez said with a sneer, "you just happened to get the same bike as Ari the day after she had hers nicked? A bike worth as much as your house, probably."

"You don't get it," I said. "I found out who stole it. Then I ... I stole it back! I went and got it off them."

Si and Ez guffawed. Yeah, that's the word, meaning a loud laugh forced out of the throat with malice.

And of course I realised how stupid it sounded. Me, finding out who had the bike and stealing it back like some kind of hero.

"But why would you even do that?" It was Ari, and I don't know if her question was about stealing the bike from her or getting it back from the gang.

I tried to say something, tried to make the right words come, but it was useless. My tongue was huge in my mouth. And now there was a big crowd around us. I looked from face to face and each one was filled with hatred or scorn.

And then I heard it, shouted from the back of the crowd. "The thief, it's Stinky Mog!"

And then, of course, it came.

Stinky Mog
Stinky Mog
He looks like a tramp
And he smells like a bog.

Si, Ez and Moll looked a bit bemused but then began laughing. My eyes went to Ari's face. She wasn't laughing. She looked like someone standing at a grave.

> *Stinky Mog*
> *Stinky Mog*
> *I'd rather snog a skunk*
> *Or a smelly dog.*

I felt my eyes begin to sting.

No, please no, not that.

But it was too late. I wiped my sleeve across my face, and it came away damp with tears and snot. There was more laughter now in the crowd. Like I said before, mine wasn't a tough school, but boys don't cry, and that's all there is to it.

And then suddenly a teacher – oh, crap, Mr Cudworth, why did it have to be him? – was there, pushing his way past, through the kids. This was the kind of situation he loved – the chance to scream and shove us around.

"What the hell's going on?" Cudworth said. "Get to your classrooms. Shift it. Move yourselves. If I see one face here in thirty seconds, it's detention for the term."

The crowd scattered.

And then he was there, looming over me. I was still on the floor.

"What is this?" Cudworth demanded. "Get up, boy. Name?"

I could see that Si was about to "explain" the situation. He moved forwards, his mouth already open, ready to call me a thief. Then Ari cut in.

"He fell, sir. We were seeing if he was all right."

Cudworth looked around the faces in the thinning crowd. Then he looked at me. I was still on the floor.

"I told you to get up, boy. What happened to you?"

"I fell, sir," I replied.

"Right, well, get off to your classes. Move it!"

The last of the crowd began to straggle away, watched by Cudworth, hands on hips. I picked myself up and followed slowly behind. I wanted to walk into a tunnel that led to the darkness at the centre of the earth. Except it's molten metal down there, isn't it? Glowing with the red of hell. Actually, that would do it.

"You all right, boy?" It was Cudworth. For some reason he wasn't yelling.

"Yes, sir."

I glanced at him. He was looking at me in a very un-Cudworth way.

"You sure?" Cudworth asked.

"Yes, sir. Fine, sir."

"OK, well, get off then. If you want any ... need any ...?"

I think he was trying to be kind. Looking at him I suddenly saw his past: a kid bullied at school, trying to make himself tough to escape it. I saw that the experience meant he could sense it in others. The fear and the loneliness. But I was beyond help. I wiped my face on my sleeve again and walked into the school.

Chapter 15

Back to the Pit

Stinky Mog had had many bad days. Days when he wanted to close his eyes and make the world go away. Days when he wanted to hurt himself to mask the deeper hurt caused by the world. Days when shame and self-loathing washed over him like a tidal wave, a tsunami of sorrow.

But he ... I mean *I* ... thought I'd left that behind. I thought I was safe. Not safe as in free, but more like I'd found a hiding place where the monsters couldn't get me.

But now Stinky Mog had been found.

The day was a horror show. Word had gone round. Everyone thought that I'd stolen Ari's bike and then, like a dumbass, turned up at school with it. And everyone saw that she'd risen above it and not grassed me up to the teachers or the police.

And because everyone loved the golden gang, everyone hated me.

Before, I'd been invisible.

Now, I was visible.

In the corridors, kids shoved me against the walls, elbowed me, spat on me. I walked into one class and every kid literally turned away as I crept to the back with my head low. The only respite came at break, when I hid in the library.

I was sitting in my favourite chair when the little round kid, Cuthbert or Colin or whatever, came up to me.

"I don't think you stole that bike," he said without any kind of introduction. "Only a psycho would do that and bring it in to school a couple of days later."

"I am a psycho," I said. "That's why I'm here with the other psychos. And losers. Like you."

Colin blinked at me a couple of times.

"I'm not good at telling when people are being sarcastic," he said, "but I think that's what you're being now."

Then I noticed that a couple of the other library geeks were hovering around. A girl with long straight black hair and a pale face, like something from a freaky horror movie. And a tall black kid. I sort of knew him. Because he was black and tall everyone thought he'd be good at sports – basketball and football and athletics. But he was useless, just like the other nerds. There was another girl, too, with curly ginger hair and thick glasses and braces on her teeth that looked like some piece of advanced military hardware.

I looked at the little group. They were like the opposite of the golden gang.

"Get lost," I said to Colin, to all of them. "Get lost and leave me alone. If I want to see losers, I'll look in the mirror."

"We're not losers," said the ginger-haired girl fiercely. "Liking books doesn't make you a loser."

I stared from face to face. All morning the faces that had looked at me had been twisted with disgust. But these kids just looked at me with hazy interest. No, not interest, that would have been OK. What I saw was sympathy. No, worse.

Pity. They pitied me.

I hated them.

I stood up and barged past them. At her desk Mrs Sunda looked at me and said, "Matthew ..." But it was too late. I was out of there.

I wasn't going to go to any more classes. No way. If I could, I'd have escaped from the school and wandered the streets. But that wasn't an option. The school was a prison, and there was no way out. The only option was my old hiding place: the hidden steps down to the boiler room.

I got there just as the bell for the end of break went off. There was drizzle in the air, but the stairway was sheltered from the worst of it. I sat hunched up on the bottom step. I felt something uncomfortable in my back pocket. It was the book that Mrs Sunda had given me. *A Kestrel for a Knave.* I looked at the cover. Some scrawny kid on it. A kid a bit like me. I tossed the book high and out of the stairwell. I threw it so far I didn't even hear it land.

Books were no use.

I remembered the times over the years I'd hidden down here. Not hidden from danger but from ... I don't know ... life, I suppose. Because life is really hard. It's hard to talk to people, hard to work out what to do. Hard to be in the world when you look terrible because you're too poor to have the stuff all the other kids have.

I thought about my mum for a while, and the feelings were so complicated you couldn't put words to them. Or, rather, you could give the feelings so many words that they cancelled each other out and turned them to noise. Like when you scrunch up the different colours of Plasticine together, and you think you're going to get a rainbow, but all you get is brown. I loved my mum, hated her, pitied her, resented her, wanted her to disappear, wanted her to be there for ever, wished she was like other mums, wished I didn't have to waste my life looking after her, needed her to need me ... All of those things and none of them. Brown Plasticine.

And I thought about Ari. It wasn't really that now I had no chance with her – I wasn't stupid, I knew I never had a chance with her – it was that now I had gone from being a nothing, something of complete unimportance, to being a totally hateful thing.

A monster.

The Minotaur.

The Minotaur only became a monster because he was hated.

You'd think that you'd get a transition stage, where a person realised you existed before they started to hate you. But I'd gone from zero to less than zero in a single day.

I stuck my knuckles into my eyes, rubbing them as hard as I could, until stars whirled and spiralled in my mind. It was one way I knew I could make the bad thoughts go away. But it didn't work. The stars couldn't drive away the mocking faces of Si and Ez and Moll and the other random, hating kids.

And down in that pit, I cried. The few tears on my face earlier on wasn't real crying. That was frustration and confusion and anger. But this was different. Now I cried properly, cried for the first time ever.

Yes, really – the first time ever.

Nothing in my years of sadness and loneliness had made me cry like this. But now it came, something huge and choking from inside me. Like I was coughing up a massive eel or worm that had been living in me. I didn't even recognise the sounds I made. They weren't like the crying you see on the telly, or when some little snot-nosed kid falls over in the street. These were raw, feral sounds. The sound of one animal being torn apart by another, deep in the jungle.

And when it finally finished, did I feel better, the way crying is said to make you feel better?

Yes and no.

Something had changed.

I'd had enough. I wasn't coming back.

This was my last day at this school.

My last day at any school.

Chapter 16

What Goes Around

I spent hours in that hole, and then I heard the bell go for the end of the day. I thought about staying down there until everyone had gone home, but I gained some courage from knowing that I wouldn't have to do any of this again, that I'd reached the end. And so I decided to walk through all the kids with my head held high. The heavy, ugly horned head of the Minotaur.

I didn't care now if they all lined up and sang the Stinky Mog song.

Screw them, screw them all.

The first mad rush for the school gates was over by the time I got there. But there was still a steady stream. A few kids nudged each other and stared, but it was mainly kids from other years, not touched in the same way by what had happened.

My plans of walking out of there with my head high soon crumpled, and I walked fast, looking at the ground in front of my feet, my hands thrust deep in my pockets. I reached the gates and was out, and I felt a surge of release. Not joy, no, nothing like that. Just a weight being lifted. I'd never have to walk back into the school, never have to listen to the song, never have to see people around me every day who were richer and happier than me and who scorned me for my dirt and poverty and unhappiness.

These weren't glorious feelings. They weren't noble or good or fine. I wasn't marching bravely to battle for justice. I was walking away. Which is just running away in slow motion.

And then I wasn't walking or running. I was flat on my arse. And there was a blinding stinging pain across my cheek. For a second I didn't know what had happened, why I was on my arse. Then my brain started working just as my mouth began to fill up with blood. I'd been punched. No, it didn't feel quite right for a punch. There wasn't enough bone in it. I'd been slapped. Slapped hard, really hard.

When I'd been shoved to the ground at the bike sheds, the horror and confusion kept me on the floor. But now I sprang back to my feet. I wasn't going to let any of the golden gang push me around any more. I'd had enough. I was going to fight back.

But when I looked up, there was no sign of the golden gang. There were a few scattered kids from our school who were either staring at me or backing away like horses spooked by a loud noise.

And it wasn't any of them that had slapped me to the ground.

Three faces: one smiling, one snarling, one blank.

Shorty.

Lanky.

Big.

I felt my insides go to mush. It felt as if I had no bones in my legs. My urge to fight back was gone. I was just fear in the shape of a kid.

Big was holding one of his hands in the other, sort of soothing it. He was the slapper. Shorty was the speaker.

"Where is it?"

I looked from face to face, still frozen by fear.

"Do you want to die?"

I shook my head. No, I didn't want to die.

"You tell us where the bike is, you don't die. You just get a beating. And that's for the trick with the bag."

"How did you ...?" I began. But I knew the answer even before Lanky laughed. The kid who'd seen me as I sped away from Brooke Towers.

"You're famous," Shorty said. "You got spied. You're Stinky Mog."

"Stinky Mog, Stinky Mog," sang Lanky, and that was a mistake.

The rage boiled back up in me. And rage gives you back your bones. I put my head down and charged at Lanky like a bull. I'm no kind of fighter. In fact, I've never had a fight. So I didn't know what to do, how to punch or dance. But Lanky wasn't expecting this. My head rammed into his guts, and he doubled over me and then fell to one side in silent, winded agony.

But I had no chance to enjoy my brief victory. I was still bent low when Big brought his meaty fist down hard on my back, and for the third time that day I was on the floor.

"Where's the bike?" said Big in a steady voice. He might have been asking when the next bus was due. I turned my face and saw that his boot was raised up right over my head, ready to stamp. I didn't care. My head was ringing from the two blows, the slap and the punch. I was hazily aware of shapes gathering round. Maybe other members of the gang. Or maybe they were just mind-shadows, my fears turned into darkness.

"Not. Your. Bike," I said. And then I said something else. A bad word. Well, three bad words. And I looked up to see an emotion for the first time on Big's fat, calm face, and I knew that the stamp was coming, and that I would never be the same person again. I was going to have no teeth, and my face was going to look like the rotten fruit left at the end of the day when the market traders went home.

Chapter 17

The Gathering

I don't know if Big's boot was really on its way down, or if that's just my memory re-ordering the universe to suit itself, but at the same moment I heard a sound – a high-pitched scream, or maybe a wail. And one of the shadows I'd seen was coming towards me, getting closer, growing. I thought it was probably one of the gang coming to join in with a kick to the guts or the face, just as Big was bringing his boot down on me.

But the shadow didn't come with a kick. The shadow burst on Big, like a wave hitting the shore. In nature, the wave doesn't move the shore, but this wave at least stopped the boot. Big rocked back, not far, but enough, and the boot never landed on my face.

I rolled away and staggered to my feet. I couldn't quite believe what I was looking at. It was Colin. He'd charged at Big and sort of bounced off him, like someone throwing a beanbag at a brick wall. And the shadows I had sensed weren't from other members of the Brooke Towers gang but the other library geeks.

"Get off him!" yelled Colin, and the others crowded round me. The ginger-haired girl, whose name now suddenly came clearly into my mind: Geraldine. The dark-haired goth, who was called Kyrie, and the tall black kid who was crap at sports, Hector. And my little Colin, of course it was Colin, with his glasses and his smooth hair. And there were others whom I really didn't know.

"Yeah, get lost!" Hector shouted.

"Clear off!" Geraldine screamed.

And other words like that. Not swear words, because this was the library gang, and they didn't swear. And somebody said, "We've told the teachers," and that sounded really feeble.

I looked at them. Six kids. Four girls, two boys. Stumpy little Year 7s and 8s. A gangly Year 9. Just the geeks. Hair in ponytails. Neat ties. Badges, their shiny badges. They all had badges. Library

Prefect. Other badges. Harry Potter stuff. Oh, god, they were doomed.

"Go away," I said to them. "You don't know what ... you're going to get ..."

I was partly thinking they were going to get hurt, mashed up by Big and Shorty and Lanky. The library geeks didn't have any experience of people like Big and Shorty and Lanky. They didn't know anything about their world. Anything about what happened there. About the darkness and the pain and the blood.

But I also didn't want them here seeing this happening to me. Didn't want them, or anyone, to be part of Stinky Mog's latest humiliation.

The Brooke Towers gang looked at each other, and then back at the nerds, and they just couldn't help but burst out laughing. Lanky was back on his feet, and you could tell that laughing hurt him where I'd butted him in the guts, but still he laughed. And you could see why. This was the lamest bunch of geeks ever assembled.

"You kids run home to Mummy," said Shorty with a smile. "Otherwise you ain't gonna be running anywhere ever again." As he said it, he put the smile away.

"Leave them," I said. "It's nothing to do with these losers. They don't know anything. They aren't even here." And then I turned to them and said, "Sod off. This isn't for you. This isn't your world. This is me."

But as I looked at them I noticed something else. More kids now were coming out of school. They were looking at us – at me and the library geeks and the Brooke Towers gang – and they were coming over. And I recognised some of the kids, recognised them because they had the glow of gold around them, like a giant halo. They were all there, there to see the end. Si and Ez and Moll and ... Ari.

She was behind the others. Wheeling the bike. Not good.

Si was always the one who tried to take control, the one who thought his job was to be in charge.

"What's this?" Si said, bustling up to us, almost like a teacher. "What's going on?"

"Go away," I said. "This is nothing to do with you."

"For once this Stinky boy has it right," said Lanky, and then he stepped forward and just hit Si with a big, wide, swinging punch. Si should have seen it coming. Should have ducked or dodged. But, like I said long ago, ours wasn't a fighting school. No one had taught him. He didn't know how to fight or to run.

Lucky for Si, Lanky was all arm and no muscle, and the punch made a slappy sound when it hit Si's face, not the crunch you get from a punch that puts you down.

But this look came on Si's face, a look of astonishment. This had never happened to him before. This thing, this brutality, this reality. His life – the lives of all the golden gang – was made of sweet and soft and nice things. And now a bitter and hard and cruel thing had come.

Somehow the Brooke Towers gang still hadn't noticed Ari and her bike. They were focused on the boys, looking for some threat, some real challenge. The library geeks were still there, puny and insignificant. The golden gang were … different. Not tough, maybe, but *there* in a way the geeks weren't.

Then I saw something else. The glint of metal.

And I knew that it had to stop, or there was going to be blood on the road.

I moved forward and said, "I told you, this is me – this is only me. This is Stinky Mog." And

I think I said it to the Brooke Towers gang, but maybe I said it to the golden gang and the library geeks.

"Yeah," said Shorty. "This boy took a bike. We come to get it back. The rest of you go. Or stay and get some hurt."

"Bike ...?"

The voice was gentle, puzzled. It was the voice of Ari.

"He stole our bike, pretty girl," Shorty said. "We come for it. End of."

And I heard a sort of noise rise from Ari and the golden gang. A breath noise but with more in it. Almost a sigh.

And I also saw Shorty's face change, a look of surprise replaced quickly by a look of joy.

"My bike!" he said, almost like a small child. A happy child.

And Ari looked at the bike and at him and at me.

"It's my bike," she said quietly.

And now I was sure this was going to end in blood.

"All of you go," I screamed.

Then I said the same thing but using other words – you know the words.

And I looked all the time at Big and Lanky and Shorty, and they looked happy enough. This was their time, their way. They'd had hard lives. When your life is hard, you become hard or you let it crush you, like I was crushed.

Was it raining? It was raining. My hair was wet, and the rain was in my eyes.

The library geeks looked scared. They huddled together in the rain. But they didn't go, they didn't run. And even the golden gang, they didn't run either. But they weren't any real use. They weren't made for this.

And then I saw something else, and my heart first flinched and shrank, and then it rose and expanded until it filled the grey sky.

It was my mum.

She was on the stupid mobility scooter. She was driving it along the pavement, towards the school. I looked and saw her face. And she looked and saw mine, and she smiled. And then I could see that she was trying to understand the situation, work out what was what, who was who.

Mum yelled out, "Matthew, Matthew!" in a voice that was clear and loud, not like any voice I'd ever heard her use before. And everyone there – the Brooke Towers gang, the golden gang, the library geeks – all looked over at her. This should have been my greatest ever humiliation, the thing I'd feared more than anything – my mum, my terrible, embarrassing, hopeless mum, being here where everyone could see. But that's not what I felt.

I felt saved.

And then Mum stopped her mobility scooter a few metres away and carefully got up from the seat with everyone gawping at her. She had her stick with her, but she hardly seemed to lean on it, and she walked over, and her walk was good and steady.

"I know you," Mum said, pointing with her stick at Big. "I know your father and your mother. And I know you," she said, this time pointing the stick at Lanky. "But I don't know you," she finished, this last time pointing at Shorty.

And somehow that was all Mum had to say. You could see the fight go out of the three of them. Somehow being known was enough to defeat the Brooke Towers gang. Or maybe it was just that she was an adult, and it's always a different thing for a kid to take on an adult, however weak. Or maybe again it was that very weakness that meant there was nothing but humiliation for them – three tough lads confronting a woman who'd just climbed off a mobility scooter. Or all of these things. They looked down, looked up, looked anywhere but at my mum. And then the Brooke Towers gang went, walking quickly away, trying to be casual but failing. Looking like children. When they were a safe distance – no, I mean a dignified distance – they looked back one more time and shouted something, some insult, some last gesture, and then they ran, literally ran.

And maybe they ran because of Mum, and maybe it was because some teachers were coming forwards through the gates. Mr Cudworth with his bluster and bravado, and a couple of other teachers, on their way home but also taking an interest in this crowd, this gathering. And there as well was Mrs Sunda, and the library geeks ran over to her and shrieked and chattered and pointed.

Mum reached me then, and she gave me an embarrassing hug. I hugged her back.

"I didn't know you could ..." I began. "I didn't know you were coming."

"Thought I'd meet you at school," Mum said. "Haven't done it for a while. Thought it'd be a surprise. Who's your friend?"

I realised that Ari was there with her bike.

"Hi, I'm Ari," she said with that easy confidence of the goldens. "I guess you're ... er ... Matthew's mum."

"Give us a sec, will you, Mum?" I said. My mum gave me a meaningful look and walked away a few metres, where she was met by Mrs Sunda, who took her hand and smiled. Most people had drifted off now. The geeks were still there, and the goldens. Moll and Ez were comforting Si, who was holding his hand to his punched face. And for a few seconds it was just Ari and me.

"I want to say ... sorry," Ari said in that voice like birdsong. "And thanks. I understand what you did. It was ... amazing."

This was only the second time she'd ever talked to me. And it was the closest I'd ever been to her.

"Earlier, I tried to explain," I said. "It was ... for you."

And then a light came into her eyes.

"The poem," Ari said. "Did you write the Minotaur poem? For my birthday ...?"

I didn't say anything. I was blushing.

"It was beautiful."

And then Ari did something I really wasn't expecting. She kissed my cheek.

Chapter 18

The Geeks

I know what you think.

You think that this is one of those stories with a happy ending, where the boy gets the girl. But life isn't like that. Life isn't one of those stories.

But the ending isn't sad, either.

I didn't end up going out with Ari. She became a sort of mate, and we'd say hi around the school and chat sometimes. And I found out that I was right about her not being rich like the other goldens, and that her dad really had scrimped and saved to get the bike, and that the loss of it had been devastating, and the recovery the greatest thing that had ever happened to her. And she was OK. Nice. Fine. Pretty, always pretty.

And the other goldens were polite to me. Si and Ez and Moll.

But there was a deeper truth. They weren't like me. Their world touched mine, but the overlap was so slight, even with Ari, that we could never be easy together. The things they knew weren't the things I knew.

But there were other things in my life.

Yeah, the geeks. I stopped fighting it. I learned all their names, not just Colin and Geraldine and Kyrie and Hector but also Mark and Mo and Kamilla and Randeep and Martina and Petyr. I didn't sit on my own in the library any more – I sat with them. I even started to wear a damn badge. Don't laugh. Mine said "Book Wizard 1st Class". I told you not to laugh!

I didn't care that we were the uncoolest kids in the school. When I needed them, the geeks had come to save me, and I loved them.

And then there was my mum. She was trying really hard. Trying to look after herself, trying to make sure we both got the help we needed. And because she was better able to take care of herself, I was able to take care of *myself*. She filled in the right forms so we had a bit more money. I wasn't hungry any more. I wasn't dirty any more. The hot water got fixed. There was soap and shampoo. My clothes still came from charity shops, but at least they fitted me and were clean, more or less. Life was still hard, really hard. My mum had some lapses. But she'd done something amazing. She'd come back from the edge, back from the ... what's it called ...? The abyss.

And she'd done it for me.

Matthew.

Farewell Stinky Mog.

Stinky Mog was dead.

The Labyrinth was torn down. The Minotaur was unmonstered.

Author spotlight

Anthony McGowan was born in Manchester in 1965 and was brought up in Yorkshire. The secondary school he went to was tough and violent, but it gave him the stories and characters he's been writing about ever since. He grew up to try out lots of different jobs – he's been a nightclub bouncer, a civil servant and a university tutor.

McGowan's first novel for young people was *Hellbent*, a dark comedy about a teenage boy who dies and goes to hell. He's also written books about a boy with a talking brain tumour, knife crime and rescuing wild animals. Most of his books are a mixture of comedy and serious ideas and issues, such as bullying and mental illness.

McGowan didn't read much fiction when he was younger, but he was obsessed with nature. One of his favourite books was *The Guinness Book of Animal Facts and Feats*. Then a teacher gave him a copy of *The Lord of the Rings*, the famous fantasy novel by J. R. R. Tolkien. He says: "It took me several years to finish reading it, but afterwards, I'd become a different kind of person; one who read novels and might one day write one."

McGowan now lives in London with his wife, two children and a dog called Monty. He has won many awards for his writing, including the Carnegie Medal, the oldest and most prestigious award for children's literature, for *Lark*.

Background to the novel

The Minotaur and Ariadne

The Minotaur was a monstrous mythical creature with the body of a man and the head and tail of a bull. King Minos of Crete imprisoned the Minotaur in the middle of a maze, or labyrinth. Theseus – a young Greek hero – offered to kill the monster. Minos's daughter, Ariadne, helped Theseus and sailed away with him afterwards, but then he left her alone on a remote island.

Matthew feels he has a lot in common with the Minotaur. He feels as though his life has made him into a monster, someone that everyone keeps away from. He sometimes hides in the space outside the school boiler room or in the library. He also has the idea that the Minotaur is the one who truly loves Ariadne, influenced by the fact that he is in love with an Ariadne of his own ("Ari").

Young carers

When we first meet Matthew, he is a young carer. The NHS describes a young carer as someone who is under 18 and who helps to look after a relative with a disability, illness, mental health condition, or drug or alcohol problem.

Young carers can get help and support from friends, family, teachers and doctors, but life can be very hard for them, like it is for Matthew. He worries about his mum and he looks after her, helping her move around, doing the shopping and cooking. By the end of the story, his mum is starting to feel better and take care of herself and Matthew.

Child poverty

Matthew and his mum don't have very much money and sometimes that means Matthew is hungry and doesn't have clean clothes that fit him. According to the Child Poverty Action Group, around 30% of children in the UK live in poverty: that's nine children in every class of 30 who live in families who earn less than 60% of the average income. They might not always have enough money for food, clothing and trips out, and their homes might be cold. Lone-parent families, like Matthew and his mum, are even more likely to face poverty.

Neglect

Matthew is neglected in this story. His mum isn't unkind, but she finds it difficult to make sure he has food to eat and clean clothes that fit him. Neglect is what happens to a child when their needs are not met. They might not have proper care, shelter, food, education or medicine. They might not be kept safe, and the people who look after them might ignore them or be mean, instead of loving and kind.

People who work with children are trained to spot the signs of neglect. In *I Am The Minotaur*, there is one adult who tries to reach out to Matthew – the librarian, Mrs Sunda – and in the end, his mum recovers from her illness enough to start looking after him.

Bullying

Matthew is bullied in a range of ways. At primary school, other children called him "Stinky Mog" because of his dirty clothes and because he doesn't always have hot water to wash himself. Later, in secondary school, Matthew has no real friends. Most of the students and teachers ignore him. Later in the story, the kids that Matthew calls "library geeks" stand up for him.

Bullying is when somebody physically hurts you, or verbally abuses you. It can make you feel lonely, upset, anxious and angry. Bullying is a common problem in schools and it can make life miserable. All schools have ways of dealing with bullying, but the first rule is always: if you are being bullied, tell someone.

Depression and anxiety

Matthew's mum is suffering from "depression and anxiety", which are mental health conditions. Depression is a serious illness that makes people feel sad and hopeless. People with depression sometimes have low energy levels and prefer to avoid others. They might find it impossible to carry on with normal life.

In the story, Matthew's mum has been taking anti-depressant pills for a long time and she has become addicted to them. She says: "You get to need them, even when the thing you first needed them for isn't there." Her new doctor helps by recommending talking therapy, which is when you visit a trained expert to talk about and understand your feelings.

Watership Down and *A Kestrel for a Knave*

These are the titles of books the librarian gives Matthew.

Watership Down (written in 1972) is a book by Richard Adams. It tells the story of a group of rabbits who have to run away from their warren. They have many adventures, led by brave and loyal

Hazel, who gets his friends out of many tricky situations.

A Kestrel for a Knave is another famous novel, written by Barry Hines in 1968. It's been made into a play and a film. The story is about a boy called Billy who has a difficult life at home and school. He rescues a kestrel and looks after it, but there is no happy ending. One of the characters in *A Kestrel for a Knave* is Mr Sugden, a bullying PE teacher a bit like Matthew's teacher, Mr Cudworth.

Gangs

In Matthew's school, there are a few groups and gangs, including the golden gang, and the geeks who hang out in the library. Being part of a group, like a friendship group or a sports team, can give us a sense of belonging and connection, while being on the outside can make us feel excluded or lonely.

Outside Matthew's school, there is the Brooke Towers gang who steal Ari's new bike. The police usually define a gang as a group of people who are involved in criminal activity or violence.

Who's who in this novel

Matthew (also called Stinky Mog) is the main character. He refers to himself as the Minotaur. He is his mum's carer and is a lonely boy who fancies a girl called Ari.

Matthew's mum suffers from depression and often has trouble looking after herself and Matthew.

Mr Cudworth is a PE teacher who punishes students who aren't sporty.

Ari, Si, Moll and Ez are a group of friends. Matthew calls them the golden gang because he thinks they are rich and have easy lives.

Mrs Sunda is the school librarian, who is kind to Matthew.

The Brooke Towers gang is a group that steals Ari's new bike. Matthew calls the place the gang is named after "the no man's land that different gangs fought over".

The geeks are Colin, Geraldine, Kyrie, Hector and others, a group who hang out in the school library.

What to read next

The Family Tree by Mal Peet

A short but powerful story about a dad who hides away from his family.

The Savage by David Almond

Part novel, part graphic novel – a story about bullying and stories coming true.

Thornhill by Pam Smy

A story about a house with secrets, told in words and powerful black and white images.

The Fall by Anthony McGowan

When Mog feels threatened by a new boy in school, he takes drastic action. A short, tense novel.

Brock, Pike, Rook and Lark by Anthony McGowan

Four stories full of danger and humour about teenager Nicky and his brother, Kenny, who has learning difficulties. Mog is the name of a minor character in Pike.

What do you think?

1. Matthew is often lonely at school. Have you ever been lonely or offered friendship to someone who needed it?

2. Mrs Sunda gives Matthew two books. How can books help when life is difficult?

3. Find out about the books *Watership Down* and *A Kestrel for a Knave*. Why do you think Mrs Sunda thought these books might be right for Matthew?

4. Matthew's mum finds it hard to look after him. Is it possible for a parent to be perfect?

5. The golden gang seem to have perfect lives, but Ari turns out to be quite ordinary. Would being rich solve all problems?

6. Matthew wants to be a hero by getting Ari's bike back. What does it take to be a true hero?

7. Being part of a group can be great fun, but it can sometimes go wrong. What would you do

if your friends wanted you to do something you knew to be wrong?

8. Matthew tells the library geeks to "Get lost and leave me alone". Why do you think he behaves this way towards them?

9. The first chapter is written in the third person, using "he" not "I". Why do you think the author has done this?

10. The shopkeeper tries to help Matthew: "And one special time the man put in a bunch of grapes that were going bad ..." (page 3). Who are the kindest and least kind adults in the story? Why do you think this?

11. Matthew sees himself as a monster, like the Minotaur. Are monsters born? Or are they made by the way people treat them?

Word list

abyss: deep, maybe bottomless, hole

bluster and bravado: angry talk and display of bravery

botoxed: treated with Botox, a substance injected to remove wrinkles

caressing: stroking

conspicuous: obvious, easy to notice

derailleur: a gear on a bicycle

dignified: serious, deserving respect

draping: hanging

eel: a long, thin snake-like fish

feeble: weak

feral: wild, savage

frisky: playful, full of energy

government cuts: reductions in the money given out by the government

lanky: tall and thin

loitering: standing or waiting around

melded: blended, joined

peril: danger

petered out: faded away

quad: short for quadrangle, a square outside space

radiation: powerful and dangerous rays, usually of radioactive substances

resented: felt bitter about

savouring: enjoying the taste of

self-loathing: a feeling of hating yourself

shrink: slang for a psychiatrist or doctor who specialises in mental health

skulking: hiding, moving secretively

small fry: unimportant people

Super-Readable
ROLLERCOASTERS

Super-Readable Rollercoasters are an exciting new collection brought to you through a collaboration between Oxford University Press and specialist publisher Barrington Stoke. Written by bestselling and award-winning authors, these titles are intended to engage and enthuse, with themes and issues matched to the readers' age.

The books have been expertly edited to remove any barriers to comprehension and then carefully laid out in Barrington Stoke's dyslexia-friendly font to make them as accessible as possible. Their shorter length allows readers to build confidence and reading stamina while engaging in a gripping, well-told story that will ensure an enjoyable reading experience.

**Other titles available in the
Super-Readable Rollercoasters series:**

Edgar & Adolf by Phil Earle and Michael Wagg
Lightning Strike by Tanya Landman
Rat by Patrice Lawrence
Dark Peak by Marcus Sedgwick

Free online teaching resources accompany all the titles in the Super-Readable Rollercoasters series and are available from:

http://www.oxfordsecondary.com/superreadable